Claire Lees Ingham is a writer of fiction and magazine articles, and an MA graduate of the famous school of writing at The University of East Anglia. She is also the executive producer of several TV drama series including *Inspector George Gently, Silent Witness, Shameless, Moonfleet* and *Waterloo Road.*

Claire grew up on the street where LS Lowry had his final home, *The Elms*. The story of *Ann Hilder* was inspired by seeing paintings being removed from the artist's house after his death, when she was six years old....

Ann Hilder

A Short Story

Claire Lees Ingham

Copyright © 2024

All rights reserved by Red Room Publishing and Claire Lees Ingham.

No part of this publication may be reproduced, distributed, or transmitted in any form or by any means, including photocopying, recording, or other electronic or mechanical methods, without the author's prior written permission, except in the case of brief quotations embodied in critical reviews and certain other non-commercial uses permitted by copyright law.

Front Cover Image: LS Lowry

Portrait of Ann 1957 (detail)

© The Lowry Collection, Salford

For Mum,

who taught me to love words,

B*efore* every enchantment there is a moment when the air grows still. Time lapses; the universe falls silent, and in that instant there is light and colour and magic everywhere you look.

I am six years old, and I am on my way to ballet class at the Congregational Hall in Mottram. My face is muffled in a red, hand-knitted scarf; my hands tucked into woollen mittens against the cold. We have already walked up the hill, past the fossilised frog in the high rock walls of the cutting, and my legs are itching inside the thick, black nylon of my ballet tights.

"Stop fidgeting about, we'll be late."

I am holding onto my mother's fingers and she is hurrying, head down, her breath streaming into the cold air like cigarette smoke. Yet, as we round the corner towards the crossroads, her stride falters and slows.

I look up at her, surprised and then follow her gaze to the commotion ahead.

"Will you look at that?"

A handful of people has gathered outside one of the dark stone houses. At the kerb a Securicor van stands with its rear doors thrown wide like a shout. Men in overalls are hurrying to and fro, loading strange, flat parcels draped with rags.

"Not even in the ground and the vultures are already moving in."

"What is it, Mum?"

She looks down at me. "Man that lived there was a painter, love. Quite famous – called Lowry."

She pulls me towards the house, and then stops to watch for a moment amongst the gawkers. I tug away from her hand and climb onto the rim of the open gate, swaying backwards and forwards, until it swings free, and I am flying.

And that's when it happens. A man trots past me, carrying one of those strange, shrouded packages. Then the wind blows, and the dustsheet flaps aside revealing a woman in red. For a moment that red is all I can see. It dances in front of my eyes, vibrant, dangerous and alive, and the noise of the city-bound traffic fades as the world grows still.

The girl in the painting is frozen, head and shoulders flat against a white background, eyes rimmed with thick black lashes like spider's legs. Her long dark hair is parted severely in the centre of her forehead. Her skin is pale, her sulky mouth scarlet to match her sweater. It is not a kind face. It wants something from me, and I cannot look away. She is a fairy tale queen, black as ebony, red as blood. She is spellbinding. Hypnotic.

Then there is a flash of movement at the edge of my vision. The security man tugs the sheet back into place and suddenly the world snaps to attention.

I only see the painting for seconds, but I never forget that face.

That is the first time I see Ann Hilder.

She sits with her feet up, drowsing, as the house settles further on its foundations. The creaks are scarcely more than sighs these days. They are ageing together - their days set in stone. The sunlight trickles through net curtains. Dust motes float in the air. In the kitchen, a piece of ham is curling where she has left it on her plate. She cannot eat much now that the number of her outings has declined. The flowered walls are becoming the limit of her universe. She hates to venture far without cause.

Now it is a summer afternoon, and she is nodding, not expecting to be woken - until the shrill ring of the doorbell permeates her dreams.

Reluctantly she heaves herself from the chair and pads along the hall. She shouts, "Yes?" before she slides the chain.

"Ann?"

She opens the door admitting a crack of sunlight and the sliver of a face.

"Miss Ann Hilder?"

"No."

She tries to close the door again, but the stranger's foot is wedged into the gap. "Please -" she says, "You must have made a mistake."

The young woman peers in through the narrow opening. Her eyes flick over the older woman's features - noting the centre parting, the long braid. And then she says gently, "No… I don't think there's any mistake."

*

The second time I think I see her face, she's on the cover of a major auction-house catalogue. The booklet slides from its plain brown envelope, spilling the slash of red that is her mouth into my hands. For a moment the world slips off kilter. When my vision levels, I snatch up my phone.

"Jack? Hi - I see you've got a Lowry coming up for sale in a month's time. One I've not heard of. Where's it from?"

I can hear his throaty laugh along the phone line - imagine it echoing back from the panelled walls of the Modern Art Department office.

"You got the Lowry catalogue in your head, Scoop?"

"Pretty much. Come on, Jack - give. Who's the seller?"

He pauses. "The lady wants to remain anonymous."

"But you know that's great for a story." I scribble a note. "And has this mystery woman got any more Lowrys in her attic?"

"Possibly"

"So, it's a family member? His heir? – A friend perhaps?"

I picture him looking over his shoulder, scanning the room for eavesdroppers as the silence stretches between us.

"All I can tell you…" he drops his voice, knowing I am holding my breath, "…is that it's not from Carol-Ann Lowry's trust collection. In fact, it's not from any of the usual sources."

"And she brought it in herself?"

"It came to us through a solicitor. She doesn't want any publicity."

"Jack - I owe you lunch."

I make noises as if I am about to break the connection. Then, just as he thinks he's off the hook I say, "Oh, Jack … know how much it might fetch?"

"Hmnm…" he hums on one note as he thinks. "Market's up. Two six – two seven. Maybe three million on the right day."

"A rarity then?"

"I didn't say that."

"You didn't have to. They put the picture on the cover."

She leads the young woman into the parlour. She still thinks of it as a parlour. Her thoughts are still shaped in the language of her childhood - a gramophone needle set into the groove of the nineteen thirties and forties. Her furniture could be from that era too - heavy family heirlooms and hand-me-downs. Her mother's clocks line the walls like sentries, their hands stopped in distant times.

The stranger looks around awkwardly until invited to sit, then reaches into her bag for her phone. "I know your name's really Ann Hilder," she says. She pauses to tap an icon on the screen for the phone's voice recorder. "The picture up for auction, it came from you."

"Did it?"

The young woman appears to have been caught off guard. She looks about the room as if seeking encouragement in its worn contents. And then her eyes light on a painting propped carelessly on an upright piano. It shows a girl in ballet dress, her long black hair caught in a braid, her lips a scarlet slash across her face. The white background glows around the figure like a spotlight.

"You've another." The young woman rises to her feet, setting the phone - still recording - on the table, and moves across the room to look more closely.

"It's wonderful - Is it you?"

The old woman watches her, calculating, but says nothing.

At last, her visitor whirls around - "The world thinks you were a fantasy – a figment of his imagination -" Her voice is accusing,

"You know so much that could aid the scholarship of his work -"

Then, as suddenly as she has begun, she breaks off and looks at the older woman squarely. "I won't beat around the bush," she says. "I want to tell your story. I want to tell the story of Ann Hilder."

I begin my investigation on the telephone. I call everyone I have ever interviewed about Lowry's life or work. I make enquiries at galleries. I call in favours with contacts, friends - then friends of friends. The word on the street confirms that this picture is something special. It's completely unknown. A mystery.

As daylight fades, I leave my office and turn along the hall to my kitchen-living room - still carrying the catalogue reverently in my hands. Only here do I have the shelf space for my vast collection of books and auction catalogues about Lowry. I have assembled biographies, arts reviews, photographs; works about every aspect of his life. The number of experts grows each year, yet every article offers a similar assessment: That Lowry was an original painter - a man who wore his eccentricity like armour and shaped the story of his life to suit his listener.

Sometimes I wonder what he would have told me if we had met.

I wonder if I would have believed him.

I fill the kettle for tea, switch on the lamp, and search the shelves until I find a tattered scrapbook. Its sugar-paper pages are overflowing with postcard reproductions of Lowry's work, and when I set the book down beneath the light, I remember that each painting is titled in green felt-tip. This is, after all, a collection begun when I was seven.

Leafing my way through the pages, I see Lowry's famous street scenes peopled with hurrying figures - children, misfits, oddly balanced, five-legged dogs. In the background, houses are strung together by lines of washing, and factories glower behind high walls like prisons - the gatehouses of hell.

At last, I find what I am looking for. The portraits. Heads and shoulders of haunted men, their cheekbones hollowed out by the light. One man stares out at me with terrifying red eyes – the image of a thousand childhood nightmares - and I turn the page quickly until I see a woman with a black braid and a sulky scarlet mouth. Her pullover is a gash of red against white. This is Lowry's 'Portrait of Ann'.

I push the catalogue aside a little, to clear a space as the kettle reaches the boil.

When I return with tea, I look down and see the cover framed against a sheaf of loose scrapbook pages. And as I stare, I know there is no doubt. The picture sent for auction is another portrait of Ann: Lowry's dream woman.

Ann Hilder.

She sits, watching, as her visitor prowls about the room. There is little now that would identify her as the girl in the painting. Her mouth is still a little sulky, but the dark eyes are clouded. Her hair is coarse, streaked with white and black. When she brushes it before her dressing mirror at night, it reminds her of grooming her mother's cat.

"How did you find me?" she asks at last.

"You certainly didn't make it easy. The breakthrough was deciding that you must exist. The rest was detective work - and luck."

The journalist returns to the sofa and sits – leaning forwards to check the voice recorder is still running. She seems pleased with herself. This cat has found the cream.

Outside, the summer afternoon has begun to fade into evening. The shouts of the local children playing seem very far away.

The old woman wonders whether now is the time to tell this story.

She wonders if the journalist has caught her.

She realises she may have to move on.

"No trace of you was ever found at Lowry's house," the journalist continues. "Relatives - friends who'd never heard about you, came to believe you were a fantasy - the pitiable invention of a lonely old man."

The young woman settles back into her chair, "After he died, why didn't you set the record straight? Why did you never come forward? Why sell the painting now?"

She talks late into the evening, until the shadows grow around them, and the dust settles with the dark. She shapes the tale from her beginning, until his end - and then her voice grows cracked and dull.

At last, she looks up and is startled to see the journalist's face bears the silvery mark of tears.

"He's been dead for so many years -" she says. "Why should this matter to you?"

"Because I have loved Lowry's work all my life," the journalist replies simply. "Because I always hoped he knew love and didn't have to pretend."

The house seems to be listening. It creaks, gently, as the old woman hesitates - shifts in her chair. Then she heaves herself forwards and says, "Come with me."

The studio is lined with canvases. They stand on the floor, their faces pressed against the walls. In the corner a worktable is cluttered with paint and discarded brushes. She bends painfully, one hand out to steady her, and then begins to turn the canvases around. The wallpaper beneath her fingers is peeling. The room smells of damp and linseed oil. But the journalist's attention is fixed on those shifting squares of paint. She gasps as picture after picture is revealed.

At length, the old woman straightens and shuffles back to view the effect.

"He called them his Coppélia series," she says.

"And they're all of you?" The young woman stares, then walks around the walls drinking in the light and colour of Lowry's work.

"We went to see the ballet many times. It was our favourite. I trained for the dance, and so he painted me."

"And no-one else has seen these, until now?"

"I wanted you to see them." As the old woman looks around her eyes sparkle and she nods, "I think he would have wanted you to see them too."

After I leave the house it is a long time before the universe becomes real. I float from pavement to car. I slip effortlessly through the late-night traffic, and the rain is no more than a streak of red taillights across my windscreen.

Once home, I spend all night listening to my recordings, transcribing the solution to Lowry's last mystery. At dawn, I fall into bed dreaming of book deals and documentaries. And when I sleep, I see Lowry's painting of the man with the red eyes – his self-portrait – and he is smiling.

It is early on the day of the auction when Jack calls me. "That article you've been hinting at – when is it due to go to press?"

I can hear the panic in his voice and I am suddenly wide-awake. I roll out of bed, my eyes darting to the manuscript - to the day outside. "Later, after the sale - Why?"

"Stop it"

"What?"

"Tell them to spike it. The man who authenticated the picture – he's changed his mind…" I hear his quick intake of breath. "…The Lowry's a fake."

"No." The world tilts suddenly and I press my back against the wall as the floor lurches beneath my feet. I am drowning - I cannot catch my breath.

Jack's voice has shattered into pieces. "I'm sorry," he says. "It's true."

"But how…?"

"It's his technique - the materials are right – but they don't believe it's his hand. They're saying it may have been a copyist – a forger. At best, an apprentice"

"There's no evidence Lowry ever had a student - not one who used his style anyway."

"There's no evidence Ann Hilder ever existed either."

The studio is empty now; the house stripped of her possessions. She glances around one last time to check. There must be no clues. No trail left to follow.

She knows her painting will be lost, but she is free.

That their story has been told is enough.

When at last she closes the door behind her, she is satisfied Lowry would have approved.

It is nearly a year later when Jack invites me to the ballet. He has learned about my childhood lessons – has even seen family photographs of me, aged six, in a pink tutu with rouged cheeks. Now I've started writing again, he's begun to talk about us moving in together. My mother likes him. Thinks he's given me back my confidence.

The ballet is to be performed at Salford's Lowry Centre. As we enter, neither of us mentions the significance of the name. It is forbidden territory now.

We are shown to low, red seats at the end of a row - and as we sit, Jack squeezes my hand - "So, what's the story?"

"Coppélia? It's about a man who builds a mechanical doll and brings it to life." Then I say without thinking, "It was Lowry's favourite."

"Is that documented?" He looks at me and smiles - until I smile back.

I nod my head, "That part of her story, at least, was authentic."

Then the house lights dim - and as the overture begins, Jack takes my hand.

At length he asks softly, "What made you believe her?"

"I don't know. I suppose I wanted her story to be true."

The curtains swish aside, and there is a sudden flurry of activity on stage. Jack looks up and whispers, "So this is Coppélia?"

A woman in a scarlet costume has whirled into the glare of the footlights.

"No," I search my memory. "That's the model for the doll, Swanhilda" - and as I say the name, I hear 'Ann-Hilder' resound in my ears. The music fades, the air grows still, and suddenly I have that rare presentiment of enchantment.

I can feel Jack staring at me, and it seems to go on for hours.

At last, he leans across and whispers - "Have you ever wondered whether they dreamed it up between them? Whether it was a game - a truth hidden inside a lie? Lowry always did love to keep people guessing."

Someone 'shushes' us behind, and as I sink into my seat I wonder if there's something in what he says. Fragments of the woman's story shift and reform in my mind - and when I recall the Coppélia paintings no one else has seen, I feel a smile begin to grow on my face where the hope once was.

On stage, the ballerina in scarlet skips and whirls, until she is nothing but a red blur - and suddenly there is light and colour and magic everywhere I look.

Author's Note

I have read almost every book about Lowry that I have been able to find. The one I always return to, and that I feel best covers the mystery of Ann Hilder is Shelley Rohde's *LS Lowry, a Biography (1999)*

Printed in Great Britain
by Amazon